SHAKESPEARE FOR

HAMLET

HENRY THE FIFTH

JULIUS CAESAR

MACBETH

A MIDSUMMER NIGHT'S DREAM

MUCH ADO ABOUT NOTHING

ROMEO AND JULIET

THE TAMING OF THE SHREW

THE TEMPEST

TWELFTH NIGHT

SHAKESPEARE ON STAGE

AS YOU LIKE IT

HAMLET

JULIUS CAESAR

MACBETH

THE MERCHANT OF VENICE

A MIDSUMMER NIGHT'S DREAM

OTHELLO, THE MOOR OF VENICE

ROMEO AND JULIET

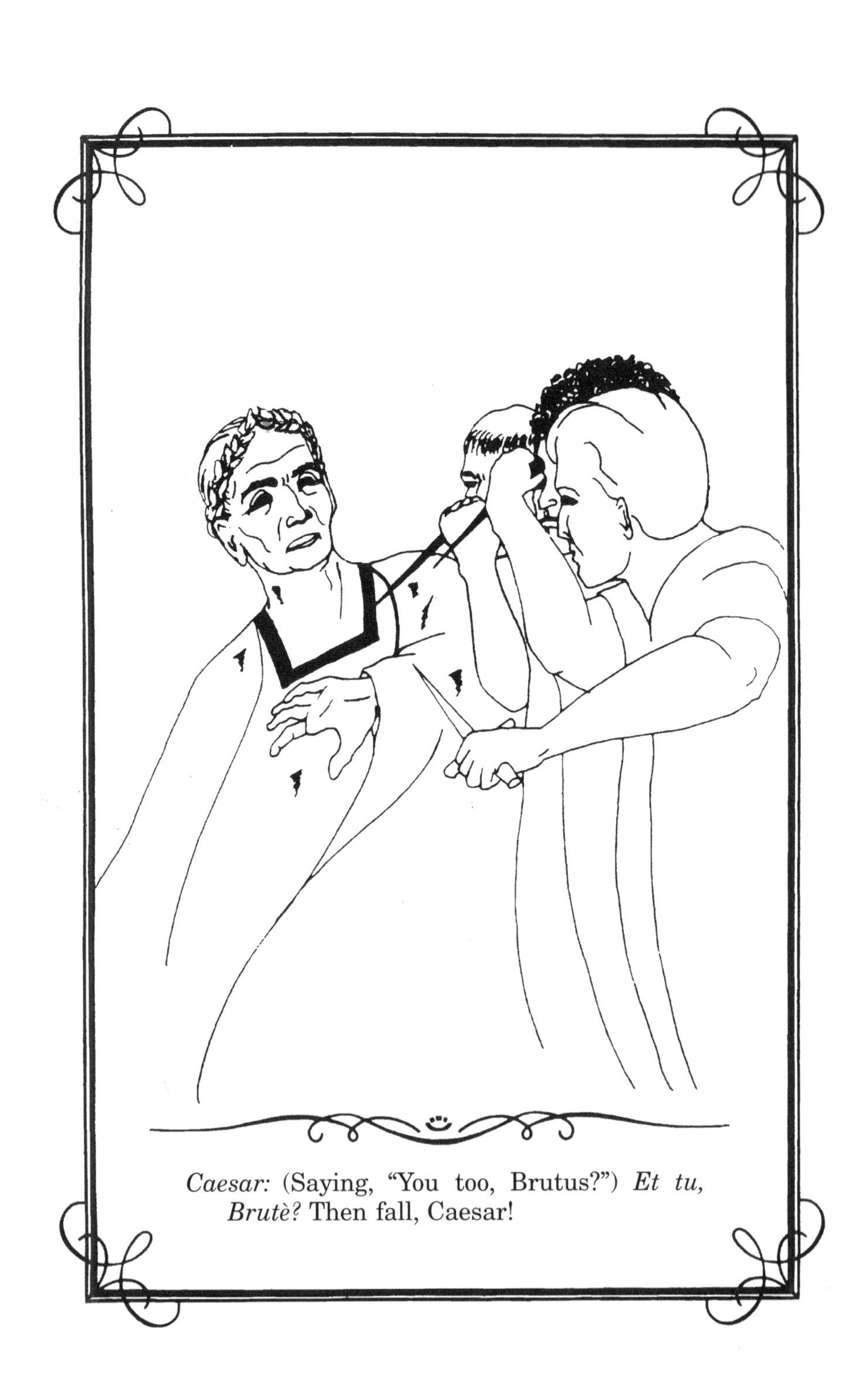

Caesar: (Saying, "You too, Brutus?") *Et tu, Brutè?* Then fall, Caesar!

SHAKESPEARE FOR YOUNG PEOPLE

JULIUS CAESAR

by
William Shakespeare

edited and illustrated by
Diane Davidson

SWAN BOOKS
a division of Learning Links Inc.
New Hyde Park, New York

Published by
SWAN BOOKS
a division of
LEARNING LINKS INC.
2300 Marcus Avenue
New Hyde Park, NY 11042

Printed in the United States of America

Library of Congress Cataloging-in-Publication Data

Shakespeare, William, 1564–1616
Julius Caesar for young people / by William Shakespeare : edited and illustrated by Diane Davidson
p. cm.—(Shakespeare for young people)

Summary: An abridged version of Shakespeare's original text, with suggestions for simple staging. Includes parenthetical explanations and descriptions within the text and announcers who summarize deleted passages.
ISBN—978-0-7675-0829-2
1. Caesar, Julius—Juvenile drama. 2. Children's plays, English. (1. Caesar, Julius—Drama. 2. Plays.) I. Davidson, Diane. II. Shakespeare, William, 1564–1616. Julius Caesar. III. Title. IV. Series: Shakespeare, William, 1564–1616. Shakespeare for young people
PR2808.A25 1990 822.3′3—dc20 90-43038

TO THE TEACHER OR PARENT

Young people can grow up loving Shakespeare if they act out his plays. Since Shakespeare wrote for the theater, not for the printed page, he is most exciting on his own ground.

Many people are afraid that young people will not understand Shakespeare's words. To help these actors follow the story, the editor has added two optional announcers, who introduce and explain scenes. However, young people pick up the general meaning with surprising ease, and they enjoy the words without completely understanding them at first. Their ears tell them the phrases often sound like music, and the plays are full of marvelous scenes.

After all, Shakespeare is not called the best of all writers because he is hard. He is the best of all writers because he is enjoyable!

HOW TO BEGIN

At first, students may find the script too difficult to enjoy, so one way to start is for the director to read the play aloud. Between scenes, he or she can ask, "What do you think is going to happen next?" or "Do you think the characters should do this?" After the students become familiar with the story and words, they can try out for parts by reading different scenes. In the end, the director should pick the actors who seem to be best, emphasizing, "There are no small parts. Everybody helps in a production." This is especially true in *Julius Caesar*, where the noisy crowd changes its mind every time a new person speaks to it.

The plays can be presented in several ways. In the simplest form, the students can read the script aloud, sitting in their seats. This will do well enough, but it is more fun to put on the actual show.

What can a director do to help the actors?

One main point in directing is to have the actors speak the words loudly and clearly. It helps if they speak a little more slowly than usual. They should not be afraid to pause or to emphasize short phrases. However, they should not try to be "arty" or stilted.

A second main point in directing is to keep the students facing the audience, even if they are talking to someone else. They should "fake front." so that their bodies face the audience and their heads are only half-way towards the other actors.

The cast should be told that when the announcers speak between scenes, servants can change the stage set, and actors can enter, exit, or stand around pretending to talk silently. But if an announcer speaks during a scene, the actors should "freeze" until the announcer has finished speaking. At no time should the actors look at the announcers. (The announcers' parts may be cut out if the director so desires.)

Encouragement and applause inspire the actors to do better, and criticism should always be linked with a compliment. Often, letting the students find their own way through the play produces the best results. And telling them, "Mean what you say," or "Be more energetic!" is all they really need.

SCHEDULES AND BUDGET

Forty-five minutes a day—using half the time for group scenes and half the time for individual scenes—is generally enough for students to rehearse. The director should encourage all to learn their lines as soon as possible. An easy way to memorize lines is to tape them and have the student listen to the tape at home each evening, going over it four or five times. Usually actors learn faster by ear than by eye. In all, it takes about six weeks to prepare a good show.

The play seems more complete if it has an audience, even another class from next door. But an afternoon or evening public performance is better yet. The director should announce the show well in advance. A PTA meeting, Open House, a Renaissance Fair, a holiday—all are excellent times to do a play.

To attract a good crowd, the admission should be very small or free. However, a Drama Fund is always useful, so some groups pass a hat, and parents sell cookies and punch. But the best way to raise money for a Drama Fund is to sell advertising in the program. A business-card size ad can sell for $5 to $10, and a larger ad brings in even more. This is money gained well in advance of the show. It can be used for costumes or small 250-500 watt spotlights that can be mounted anywhere. Until there is money in the Drama Fund, the director often becomes an expert at borrowing and improvising. Fortunately, Shakespeare's plays can be produced with almost no scenery or special costumes, and there are no royalties to pay.

SPECIAL NOTES ON THIS PLAY

Julius Caesar needs only simple staging: two "wings" or screens on each side of the playing area, with a ladder behind one to act as a platform. A bench stands at the center back. (Fig. 1)

To use as screens, tall cardboard refrigerator boxes are good. Stage flats, frames of 1″ × 4″ lumber joined by triangles of plywood and covered with muslin sheeting, are excellent if small side flats are hinged to the main one to provide bracing.

Also, two "marble" heads on pedestals help explain the central action, one bust labeled CAESAR and the other POMPEY. These can be made with wig dummies.

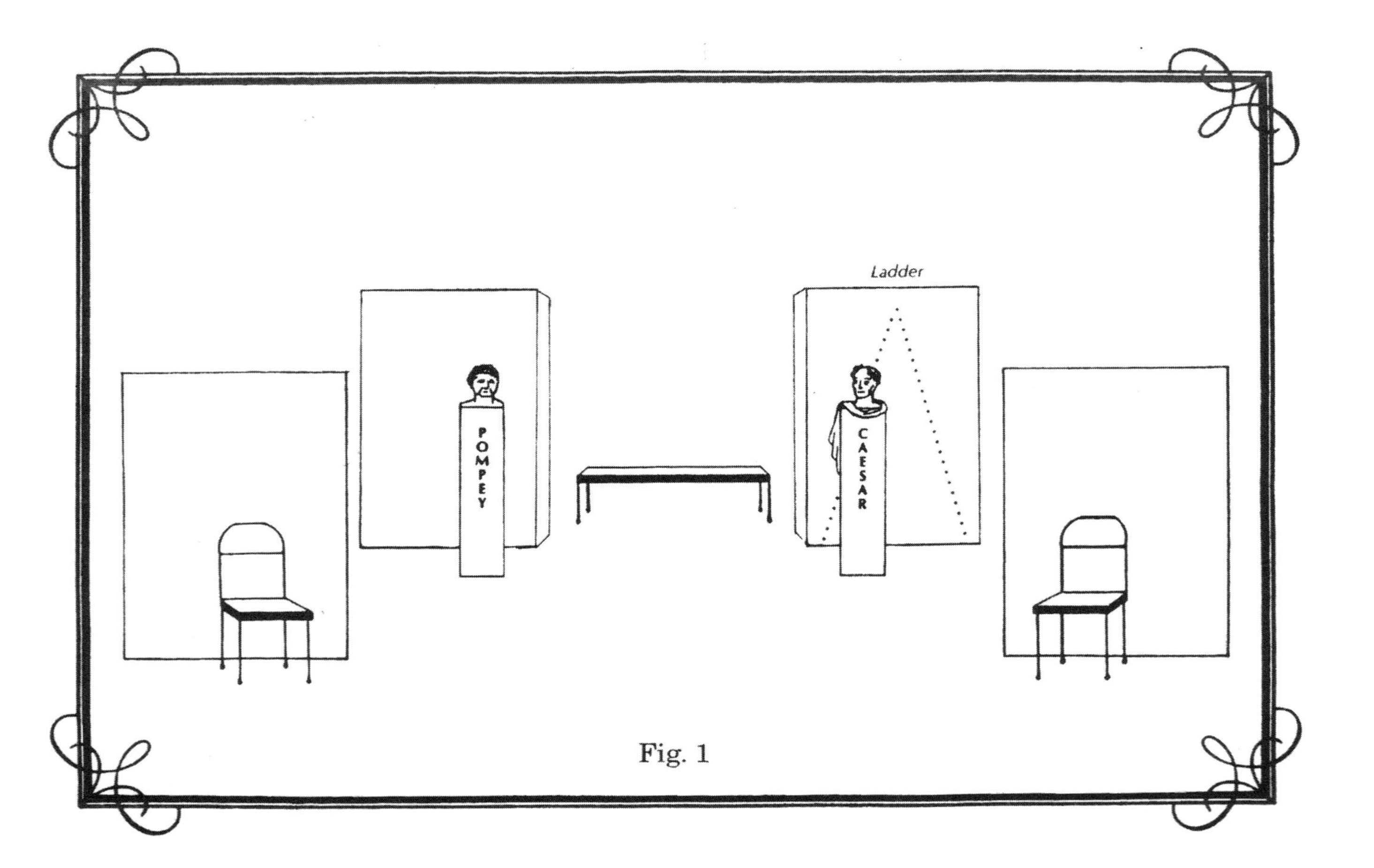

Fig. 1

In *Julius Caesar,* there are several scenes, easily indicated by simple props. On each side of the stage should be chairs, where the two announcers sit during scenes.

For *Julius Caesar*, provide simple Roman costumes for everyone: very simple long or short tunics with a cord around the waist, and a piece of cloth draped as a toga or cloak. Caesar should wear a laurel wreath. To help the audience understand the plot, it is best to have Caesar and his friends, such as Antony and Octavius, wear the same colored trim on their tunics, while Pompey's friends, such as Cassius and the other conspirators, wear another color. Brutus should have no trim until he joins the conspirators, when he could tie the appropriately colored cord around his waist as a badge.

When the murder occurs, Caesar should receive twenty-three stab wounds, made of short streamers of red crepe paper with tape on one end. These can be hidden under the murderers' togas until it is time to paste them on Caesar secretly during the action. A few more streamers could be looped to give the murderers "bloody" hands.

A word of warning is necessary: the actors should use only cardboard swords and daggers, handled carefully, so that no one is hurt. For background music, an excellent choice is the march from Verdi's opera *Aida*; for variety, plain drum beats between scenes are effective.

A LAST BIT OF ADVICE

How will a director know if the play has been produced "correctly"? He can ask his group if they had fun. If they answer, "Yes," then the show is a success!

CHARACTERS

Two Announcers (optional), who have been added

Political Party of Julius Caesar

Julius Caesar, the proud Dictator of Rome
Mark Antony, Caesar's best friend, a fine general
Octavius (Oc-**tay**-vee-us), Caesar's adopted son
Artemidorus (Ar-tee-muh-**dor**-us), a teacher
Soldiers

Former Political Party of Pompey (**Pom**-pee)

Flavius (**Flay**-vee-us) } Pompey's former officers
Murellus (Moo-**rell**-us) } Pompey's former officers
Brutus (**Broo**-tus), an honorable nobleman
Cassius (**Kas**-see-us), a clever trouble-maker
Casca (**Kas**-ka), a sour gossip
Trebonius (Tree-**bone**-ee-us), a young noble
Decius (**Dee**-see-us), a smooth-talking noble
Metellus Cimber (**Meh**-tell-us **Sim**-ber), a rebel
Cinna (**Sin**-nah), a nervous noble
Lucilius (Loo-**sill**-ee-us) } Brutus's officers
Messala (Mes-**sal**-lah) } Brutus's officers
Volumnius (Vo-**loom**-nee-us) } Brutus's officers
Clitis (**Cly**-tus) } Brutus's officers
Strato (**Stray**-tow) } Brutus's officers
Titinius (Tie-**tin**-ee-us) } Cassius's officers
Pindarus (Pin-**dah**-rus) } Cassius's officers
Soldiers

Ladies

Portia (**Por**-shah), Brutus's good wife
Calpurnia (Kal-**purr**-nee-uh), Caesar's worried wife

Romans

Cicero (**Sih**-suh-row), an important senator
A Cobbler, a shoe repairman who makes jokes
A Soothsayer, a crazy fortune-teller
Citizens, who represent the common people

Servants

Lucius (**Loo**-see-us), Brutus's sleepy servant
Servants, who move props and scenery

Characters in the Epilogue (optional)

Octavius Caesar, who becomes the Emperor Augustus of Rome
Mark Antony, the famous Roman general
Herod the Great, King of the Jews
Cleopatra, the beautiful Queen of Egypt
Clerks, secretaries to Augustus
Taxpayers

ACT I

(Two statues indicate a street in Rome. Caesar's statue is draped with purple cloth and a laurel wreath, while the statue of Pompey is plain. Two announcers enter, bow, and take their places on each side of the stage.)

Announcer 1: (To the audience) Welcome everyone to a production of Shakespeare's *Julius Caesar* given by the ___________ class.

Announcer 2: This is not the complete play but a short edition, using the original words of Shakespeare.

Announcer 1: The story begins in the Ancient Roman Republic, after a terrible civil war between two generals who wanted to lead the country.

Announcer 2: One general was Julius Caesar. *(He points to Caesar's statue.)*

Announcer 1: The other general was Pompey. *(He points to Pompey's statue.)*

Announcer 2: After a great battle, Caesar was victorious, and Pompey and his sons were killed.

Announcer 1: Today Caesar is having a victory parade called a triumph. This is also a holy day, the Feast of Lupercal.

Announcer 2: But many of Pompey's old friends are angry about Caesar's victory, and they want to stop the celebration in the streets. *(The two announcers sit.)*

(The Cobbler and Citizens come on stage, happily shouting "Hail Caesar!" and waving flowering tree branches. They throw the petals like confetti. Two Roman officers, Flavius and Murellus, stop them angrily to make them go home.)

Flavius: (Pointing offstage) Hence! Home, you idle creatures, get you home! Is this a holiday? *(To the Cobbler)* You, sir, what trade are you?

Cobbler: (He takes off his sandal and holds it out.) Truly, sir, I am a cobbler. *(He pretends to sew it.)*

Flavius: Thou art a cobbler, art thou?

Cobbler: (With a wink) I am indeed, sir, a surgeon to old shoes. *(He sews some more.)* When they are in great danger, I recover them. *(His friends laugh.)*

Flavius: But wherefore art not in thy shop today? Why dost thou lead these men about the streets?

Cobbler: (With a grin, as he puts his sandal back on again.) Truly, sir, to wear out their shoes, to get myself into more work. *(His friends laugh.)* But, indeed, sir, we make holiday to see Caesar and to rejoice in his triumph. *(All shout, "Hail, Caesar!" and throw flowers again.)*

Announcer 1: The officers are angry because the crowd used to cheer the dead leader Pompey in the same way.

Murellus: (With anger) Wherefore rejoice? You blocks, you stones, you worse than senseless things! *(He shakes his fist.)* O you hard hearts, you cruel men of

Rome! Knew you not Pompey? *(He points to Pompey's statue.)*

(The townsmen look ashamed as Murellus continues, reminding them how they admired Pompey in the past.) Many a time and oft have you climbed up to walls and battlements, to towers and windows, yea to chimney tops, your infants in your arms, and there have sat the livelong day to see great Pompey pass the streets of Rome. And when you saw his chariot but appear, have you not made an universal shout? *(The citizens nod agreement, sadly.)*

(Still scolding Murellus goes on.) And do you now cull out a holiday? And do you now strew flowers in his way . . . *(He points at Caesar's statue)* . . . that comes in triumph over Pompey's blood? *(He points again to Pompey's statue.)*

(Angrily, he pushes them off.) Be gone! Run to your houses, fall upon your knees, pray to the gods!

Flavius: (As the Citizens leave, ashamed) Go, go, good countrymen. *(After the men depart, Flavius turns to his partner and points in another direction.)* Go you down that way towards the Capitol. *(He points the way the Citizens left.)* This way will I. *(He removes the purple cloth and laurel wreath from Caesar.)* Disrobe the images.

Murellus: (Worried) May we do so? You know it is the Feast of Lupercal.

Flavius: (Shrugging) It is no matter. Let no images be hung with Caesar's trophies. *(As they leave, he goes back and puts the wreath on Pompey's head.)*

(There is loud music or a drum, and proud Caesar parades with his wife Calpurnia and friend Mark Antony, who is warming up for the sacred Lupercal race by jogging in place. Two other men warm up also. A large crowd follows to watch, including Cassius, Casca, and the Soothsayer. Mark Antony notices the wreath on Pompey's statue and quietly puts it back on Caesar's statue. The runners get set, and Caesar raises his hand as a signal.)

Announcer 2: Caesar's celebration begins with a religious race, but it is soon interrupted.

Caesar: (Loudly) Set on, and leave no ceremony out.

(As he lowers his hand, the runners dart off. Everyone cheers. But through the cheers comes a strange voice crying out from the crowd.)

Soothsayer: Caesar!

Caesar: (Turning haughtily) Ha! Who calls?

Casca: Bid every noise be still. Peace yet again! *(The crowd grows quiet.)*

Caesar: (Looking about) Who is it that calls on me? I hear a tongue shriller than all the music cry, "Caesar!" Speak! Caesar is turned to hear. *(In the middle of the crowd the Soothsayer, looking crazed, raises his hand in warning.)*

Announcer 1: A Soothsayer, a kind of fortune teller, warns that the fifteenth day of March, called the ides of March, will be dangerous.

Soothsayer: (Slowly, in a dreadful voice) Beware . . . the . . . ides . . . of . . . March. *(The crowd gasps.)*

Caesar: (Still not seeing the Soothsayer) What man is that? Set him before me. Let me see his face.

Cassius: (Pulling the Soothsayer forward) Fellow, come from the throng. Look upon Caesar.

Caesar: (Frowning at the stranger) Speak once again.

Soothsayer: (With a wild gesture) Beware . . . the . . . ides . . . of . . . March! *(He gives an insane laugh.)*

Caesar: (Nervously making a joke of the situation) He is a dreamer. Let us leave him. Pass!

(Everyone laughs, and with great ceremony and drumbeats, all march off after Antony to see the running. Only Brutus and Cassius are left alone, quietly pretending to talk in front of Pompey's statue, while the announcers speak.)

Announcer 2: Cassius, a troublemaker who used to be one of Pompey's men, tries to stir up his good brother-in-law Brutus to rebellion.

Announcer 1: He hints that Caesar, who has already been declared a god, might want to be a king.

Announcer 2: Rome had many gods, but they hated kings because hundreds of years earlier some kings were bad rulers. A famous ancestor of Brutus was the hero who killed the last Roman king and helped start the Roman Republic.

Announcer 1: The people of Rome consider the title of "King" to be wicked, and a crown represents evil.

Cassius: (To Brutus as he looks after the race.) Will you go see the order of the course?

Brutus: Not I. I am not gamesome.

Cassius: Good Brutus, be prepared to hear . . . *(But a loud cheer comes from Caesar's crowd offstage. Both and Cassius frown at the noise.)*

Brutus: What means this shouting? I do fear the people choose Caesar for their king.

Cassius: (Alertly) Ay, do you fear it? *(With a hint, he takes hold of Brutus's arm.)* Then must I think you would not have it so.

Brutus: (Shaking his head with a frown.) I would not, Cassius; yet I love him well. *(He changes the subject and removes Cassius's gripping hand.)* But wherefore do you hold me here so long? What is it you would impart to me? *(Hoping to hear of honorable public causes)* If it be aught toward the general good, I love the name of honor more than I fear death.

Cassius: Well, honor is the subject of my story. *(Brutus looks interested to hear of honor, but Cassius starts complaining about Caesar instead.)* I was born free as Caesar, so were you. *(Brutus nods.)*

Announcer 2: Cassius reveals Caesar's weakness by telling about the time he had to save him from drowning.

Cassius: For once upon a raw and gusty day, Caesar said to me, "Darest thou, Cassius, now leap in with me into this angry flood, and swim to yonder point?". Upon the word, I plunged in and bade him follow. So indeed he did. But Caesar cried, "Help me, Cassius, or I sink!" *(With a jealous sneer, he points at Caesar's statue.)* And this man is now become a god.

(From offstage comes a second cheer for Caesar. Both Brutus and Cassius look worried.)

Brutus: Another general shout. I do believe that these applauses are for some new honors that are heaped on Caesar.

Announcer 1: Cassius compares Caesar to a giant statue that makes everyone else look like a dwarf.

Cassius: (Bitterly, gesturing towards Caesar) Why, man, he doth bestride the narrow world like a Colossus, and we petty men walk under his huge legs and peep about to find ourselves dishonorable graves.

Announcer 2: Cassius adds that men should rule themselves. Their problem is not their unlucky stars but their own weakness.

Cassius: Men at some time were masters of their fates. The fault, dear Brutus, is not in our stars, but in ourselves, that we are underlings.

Announcer 1: Cassius hints that Brutus should be leader of Rome.

Cassius: (Softly) Brutus and Caesar . . . Why should that name be sounded more than yours? *(He takes the laurel wreath from Caesar's statue and puts it on Brutus's head.)* Yours is as fair a name.

Brutus: (Stopping any further talk, he takes off the wreath and looks at it.) What you have said, I will consider. What you have to say, I will with patience hear. Till then, my noble friend, chew upon this; Brutus had rather be a villager than a son of Rome under these hard conditions. *(He throws the wreath down sadly.)*

(Caesar's group enters suddenly, but everyone seems upset. Caesar is very angry.)

Brutus: The games are done, and Caesar is returning. But look you, Cassius. The angry spot doth glow on Caesar's brow.

Cassius: Casca will tell us what the matter is.

Announcer 2: Suddenly the angry Caesar thinks Cassius is a troublemaker.

Caesar: (Taking Antony to one side) Antonio.

Antony: Caesar.

Caesar: Let me have men about me that are fat. *(He points at skinny Cassius.)* Yon Cassius has a lean and hungry look. He thinks too much. Such men are dangerous.

Antony: (Cheerfully) Fear him not, Caesar. He's not dangerous. He is a noble Roman.

Caesar: I fear him not. He reads much. He loves no plays, as thou dost, Antony. He hears no music.

Seldom he smiles, and smiles in such a sort as if he mocked himself. Such men as he are very dangerous.

With a flourish of music, Caesar and his friends leave, except for Casca, a grouchy fellow whom Cassius has stopped.)

Announcer 1: Cassius wants to know about the shouting and about Caesar's angry looks.

Casca: (To Cassius in a grumbling voice) You pulled me by the cloak. Would you speak with me?

Brutus: Ay, Casca. Tell us what hath chanced today that Caesar looks so sad.

Casca: (Scornfully) Why, there was a crown offered him; and being offered him, he put it by with the back of his hand, thus. *(He shows how Caesar pushed the crown away.)* And then the people fell a-shouting.

Brutus: (Alarmed at the idea of a crown.) What was the second noise for?

Casca: (Roughly) Why, for that, too.

Cassius: They shouted thrice. What was the last cry for?

Casca: (More roughly) Why, for that too.

Brutus: (Shocked) Was the crown offered him thrice?

Casca: (Nods) Ay, and he put it by thrice . . . *(He makes the same gesture again)* . . . every time gentler than other. *(He scoffs at Caesar's weak refusals.)* And at every putting-by, mine honest neighbors shouted.

Cassius: (Angrily) Who offered him the crown?

Casca: Why, Antony. It was mere foolery.

Cassius: (Eagerly) Did Cicero say anything?

Casca: Ay, he spoke Greek.

Cassius: To what effect?

Casca: Nay, for mine own part, it was Greek to me. I could tell you more news too. *(He points to Caesar's statue.)* Murellus and Flavius, for pulling scarfs off Caesar's images, are put to silence. *(He cuts his throat with his finger to show their death.)* Fare you well. *(He leaves.)*

Brutus: (Awkwardly, to Cassius) For this time I will leave you. Tomorrow, if you please to speak with me, I will come home to you; or if you will, come home to me, and I will wait for you.

Cassius: I will do so. *(With meaning he picks up the laurel wreath and puts it back on Caesar's statue.)* Till then, think of the world. *(He watches Brutus leave and then exits also.)*

Announcer 2: A month later, the night before the ides of March, all of Rome is frightened by a terrible earthquake and storm.

Announcer 1: Weird things have been seen.

Announcer 2: Romans believed that such strange events foretold the death of a ruler like Caesar.

(Thunder roars and lightning flashes as Casca and Cicero enter from different directions.)

Cicero: (Calmly) Good even, Casca. *(Casca roughly waves a sword as if to protect himself.)* Why are you breathless, and why stare you so?

Casca: (Looking about as if he feels an earthquake) Are not you moved, when all the earth shakes? *(He points to the sky filled with lightning flashes.)* O Cicero, never till now did I go through a tempest dropping fire.

Cicero: (Very amused) Why, saw you anything more wonderful?

Casca: (Frightened by unnatural sights) I have not since put up my sword. *(He points behind him.)* Against the Capitol, I met a lion who glared upon me and went by without annoying me. *(He adds more news roughly.)* A hundred ghastly women swore they saw men, all in fire, walk up and down the streets.

Cicero: (A little uneasy himself) Indeed, it is a strange-disposed time. Good night, then, Casca. *(He looks up at the storm and shudders.)* This disturbed sky is not to walk in. *(He exits.)*

Casca: Farewell, Cicero. *(He continues on his way, frightened, and almost bumps into Cassius, who enters. They spring apart in the darkness.)*

Cassius: Who's there?

Casca: A Roman.

Cassius: (Coming to shake hands) Casca, by your voice.

Casca: (With relief) Cassius, what a night is this!

Cassius: Now could I, Casca, name to thee a man most like this dreadful night, that thunders and roars as doth the lion in the Capitol.

Casca: 'Tis Caesar that you mean, is it not, Cassius?

Cassius: (Mysteriously) Let it be who it is.

Casca: They say the senators tomorrow mean to establish Caesar as a king. And he shall wear his crown by sea and land in every place save here in Italy.

Cassius: (Drawing a dagger and pretending to stab someone) I know where I will wear this dagger then.

Announcer 1: Cassius and others have planned to kill Caesar the next day, the ides of March.

Cassius: (Smiling wickedly) Now, know you, Casca, I have moved already some of the noblest-minded Romans to undergo with me an enterprise most bloody, fiery, and most terrible.

Casca: I will set this foot of mine as far as who goes farthest. *(They grip hands in agreement.)*

(Suddenly Cinna enters, and Cassius and Casca are on guard until they recognize him. Cassius lowers his weapon, and so does Casca.)

Cassius: (To Casca) 'Tis Cinna. He is a friend. *(To the newcomer)* Cinna, where haste you so?

Cinna: To find out you.

Announcer 2: The conspirators, who plan to kill Caesar, need the honorable Brutus to join them to make them look respectable.

Cinna: (Nervously) O Cassius, if you could but win the noble Brutus to our party.

Announcer 1: They plan to send Brutus anonymous letters, urging him to start a revolution.

Cassius: (Giving him a scroll) Good Cinna, take this paper and look you lay it in the praetor's chair, where Brutus may but find it. *(He gives him another.)* And throw this in at his window. *(Cinna takes the scrolls and leaves, as Cassius turns to Casca.)* Come, Casca, you and I will yet ere day see Brutus at his house. *(With hope)* Three parts of him is ours already.

Casca: (With a snort of agreement) O, he sits high in all the people's hearts.

Cassius: Let us go, for it is after midnight, and ere day we will awake him and be sure of him. *(They leave, determined to have Brutus join them.)*

ACT II

(Servants take off the two statues and bring on a small potted tree. Cinna appears long enough to throw two or three scrolls onto the scene before leaving nervously. Brutus enters, picks one up, sits on the bench, and reads the scroll, frowning.)

Announcer 1: That same night, Brutus sits in his orchard garden, worried about Caesar's ambition.

Announcer 2: Brutus does not know what to do because Caesar has not yet become a king.

Announcer 1: This is the problem—should Caesar be killed just in case he might turn bad?

Brutus: (To himself) It must be by his death. *(He thinks how Caesar might act.)* He would be crowned. How that might change his nature, there's the question. Crown him; and then I grant we put a sting in him that he may do danger with. *(He shakes his head, worried.)* And therefore think him as a serpent's egg, which, hatched, would as his kind grow mischievous, and kill him in the shell.

Lucius: (A young servant enters with another scroll.) In your closet, sir, I found this paper.

(There is a loud knocking offstage. Lucius goes to see what it is.)

Brutus: (Reading the paper) "Brutus, awake. Shall Rome, etc. Speak, strike." *(He shakes his head, puzzled.)* Am I entreated to speak and strike? *(Lucius returns.)*

Lucius: Sir, tis your brother Cassius at the door.

Brutus: Is he alone?

Lucius: No, sir, there are more with him. Their hats are plucked about their ears, and half their faces buried in their cloaks.

Brutus: Let 'em enter. *(Lucius shows in Cassius, Casca, Decius, Cinna, Metellus, and Trebonius, their slouch hats pulled down and their togas muffled about their faces so they look like spies.)*

Cassius: Good morrow, Brutus. *(They shake hands.)*

Brutus: (Looking at the others) Know I these men that come along with you?

Cassius: Yes. *(He names the men as Brutus shakes hands with them.)* This is Trebonius. This, Decius. This, Casca. This, Cinna, and this, Metellus Cimber.

Brutus: They are all welcome.

Cassius: (Taking Brutus's arm) Shall I entreat a word? *(He leads him aside to talk, as the others look at the first light of dawn.)*

Decius: (Pointing at the sky) Here lies the east. Doth not the day break here?

Casca: (Gruffly) No. *(He raises his sword.)* Here, as I point my sword, the sun arises, and the high east stands as the Capitol, directly here.

(As Brutus and Cassius return to the others, Brutus takes a colored cord from Cassius and ties it about his waist. He smiles, showing he has joined them.)

Announcer 2: Brutus has decided to join the conspirators who plan to kill Caesar for the good of Rome.

Brutus: Give me hands all over, one by one. This shall be or we will fall for it? *(They shake hands.)*

Announcer 1: From now on, the conspirators will follow the noble Brutus, even though the troublemaker Cassius has better ideas.

Decius: Shall no man else be touched but only Caesar?

Cassius: (Strongly) Decius, well urged. Let Antony and Caesar fall together. *(All murmur agreement until Brutus changes their minds.)*

Brutus: (Gently correcting Cassius) Our course will seem too bloody, Cassius. Let's be sacrificers, but not butchers. And for Mark Antony, think not of him, for he can do no more than Caesar's arm when Caesar's head is off.

Cassius: (With great warning) Yet I fear him.

Trebonius: Let him not die; for he will live and laugh at this hereafter. *(The others agree though Cassius frowns, overruled.)*

Cassius: (Mentioning a new problem) But it is doubtful yet whether Caesar will come forth today or no.

Decius: Let me work, and I will bring him to the Capitol.

Cassius: Nay, we will all of us be there to fetch him. *(He looks at the sky.)* The morning comes upon us. We'll leave you, Brutus. *(After shaking hands again, he and the others exit.)*

Announcer 2: But Portia, Brutus's good wife, is worried about such strange visitors.

Portia: (Entering) Brutus, my lord, make me acquainted with your cause of grief. It will not let you eat, nor talk, nor sleep.

Brutus: (Turning away from her) I am not well in health, and that is all.

Portia: No, my Brutus. You have some sick offense within your mind I ought to know of. *(She kneels.)* Upon my knees I charm you, that you unfold what men tonight have had resort to you. *(She points after them.)* Here have been some six or seven, who did hide their faces even from darkness.

Brutus: (Helping her rise) Kneel not, gentle Portia.

Portia: I should not need, if you were gentle Brutus.

Announcer 1: Portia thinks a wife should share her husband's troubles.

Portia: Within the bond of marriage, tell me, Brutus, is it excepted I should know no secrets? Am I to keep with you at meals and talk to you sometimes? If it be no more, Portia is not his wife.

Brutus: (Kindly) You are my true and honorable wife.

Portia: If this were true, then should I know this, secret. I grant I am a woman, but withal a woman that Lord Brutus took to wife. I grant I am a woman, but withal a woman well-reputed, Cato's daughter. Think you I am no stronger than my sex, being so fathered and so husbanded? Tell me your counsels! I will not disclose 'em.

Brutus: (With a prayer to heaven.) O ye gods, render me worthy of this noble wife! *(He puts his arm about her.)* Portia, go in, and thy bosom shall partake the secrets of my heart. *(They leave together.)*

(Servants remove the tree and place a tripod on the stage to show Caesar's house. Caesar enters, frowning and pacing the floor.)

Announcer 2: At Caesar's house, both Caesar and his wife Calpurnia are worried about her bad dreams, for Romans thought dreams told the future.

Caesar: (To himself) Nor heaven nor earth have been at peace tonight. Thrice hath Calpurnia in her sleep cried out, "Help, ho! They murder Caesar!"

Calpurnia: (Entering fearfully) What mean you, Caesar? Think you to walk forth? You shall not stir out of your house today.

Caesar: (Looking brave) Caesar shall go forth.

Announcer 1: She tells of more weird signs that warn of death to a country's leader.

Calpurnia: (With horror, pointing off to the city) A lioness hath whelped in the streets. *(She looks at the sky.)* Fierce fiery warriors fight upon the clouds, which drizzled blood upon the Capitol. *(Clasping her hands in fright)* And ghosts did shriek and squeal about the streets.

Caesar: (Firmly) Yet Caesar shall go forth.

Calpurnia: (In a desperate voice) When beggars die there are no comets seen; The heavens themselves blaze forth the death of princes.

Announcer 2: But Caesar refuses to die of fright.

Caesar: (Proudly) Cowards die many times before their deaths. The valiant never taste of death but once.

Calpurnia: (Kneeling) Alas, my lord. Do not go forth today. We'll send Mark Antony to the Senate House, and he shall say you are not well today.

Caesar: (Giving in to her plea easily) For thy humor I will stay at home. *(He sees Decius enter.)* Here's Decius Brutus. He shall tell them so.

Decius: (Full of hearty smiles) Caesar, all hail! I come to fetch you to the Senate House.

Caesar: Bear my greeting to the senators, and tell them that I will not come today. *(Calpurnia rises.)*

Decius: (Smoothly covering his surprise) Most mighty Caesar, let me know some cause, lest I be laughed at when I tell them so.

Caesar: (Stiffly, rather embarrassed) Calpurnia here, my wife, stays me at home. She dreamt tonight she saw my statue, which with an hundred spouts did run pure blood. And many Romans came smiling and did bathe their hands in it. *(His wife nods, anxiously.)*

Announcer 1: Decius tricks Caesar by making the dream sound good.

Decius: This dream was a vision fair and fortunate. *(He thinks fast.)* Your statue spouting blood in many pipes signifies that from you great Rome shall suck reviving blood. *(Caesar smiles at the idea.)*

Announcer 2: Then Decius says that Caesar might look like a coward if he does not go to the Senate.

Decius: Know it now: the Senate have concluded to give this day a crown to mighty Caesar. *(Caesar looks very happy.)* If you send them word you will not come, their minds may change. *(He imitates a gossipy voice.)* "Break up the Senate till another time, when Caesar's wife shall meet with better dreams." *(With heavy mockery)* If Caesar hide himself, shall they not whisper, "Lo, Caesar is afraid"?

Caesar: (Shocked, blaming is wife for his worries) How foolish do your fears seem now, Calpurnia! Give me my robe, for I will go. *(She shakes her head.)*

(The conspirators—Brutus, Metellus, Casca, Trebonius, and Cinna—enter, their daggers underneath their robes. Antony enters also.)

Caesar: (To the newcomers) Welcome. Good morrow. We, like friends, will straightway go together. *(All leave for the Senate House, and Calpurnia watches fearfully before she, too, exits.)*

(The servants remove the tripod, putting back the two statues from the first scene.)

Announcer 1: A teacher, Artemidorus, has heard rumors of danger to Caesar. He tries to warn him.

Artemidorus: (Enters, reading from a scroll) "Caesar, beware of Brutus. Take heed of Cassius. Come not near Casca. Trust not Trebonius. Decius Brutus loves thee not. The mighty gods defend thee!" *(He looks about and places himself by Caesar's statue.)* Here will I stand till Caesar pass along, and as a suitor will I give him this. *(He rolls up the scroll carefully.)* If thou read this, O Caesar, thou mayest live. If not, the fates with traitors do contrive.

ACT III

(The scene continues, as Caesar enters with Mark Antony, followed by the nervous conspirators. A crowd of five or six people arrives to give Caesar scrolls or petitions as he walks along. It is his morning mail. All are watched by Artemidorus and the strange Soothsayer, who has put himself in Caesar's path.)

Announcer 2: It is now the fatal fifteenth day of March, the ides of March.

Caesar: (To the Soothsayer, as a scornful joke) The ides of March are come. *(He laughs lightly.)*

Soothsayer: (Raising his hands to the skies in warning.) Ay, Caesar, but not gone. *(Caesar frowns.)*

Artemidorus: (Pushing the Soothsayer to one side, he shouts.) Hail, Caesar! *(He puts his scroll into Caesar's hands.)* Read this schedule.

Decius: (Putting another scroll into Caesar's hands) Trebonius doth desire you to read his suit.

Artemidorus: O Caesar, read mine first. *(He shrieks with fear.)* Read it instantly.

Caesar: (Frowning) What, is the fellow mad? *(As Decius pushes Artemidorus away, Caesar goes to the center of the stage, close to Pompey's statue.)*

Cassius: (Nervously to Casca, who is to stab Caesar first.) Casca, be sudden, for we fear prevention.

Brutus: (Calming Cassius) Cassius, be constant.

Cassius: (With relief, as he sees Trebonius take Antony offstage, talking and smiling) Trebonius knows his time, for look you, Brutus, he draws Mark Antony out of of the way.

Announcer 1: The conspirators will not wait for the Senate to crown Caesar. They will kill him now.

Caesar: (Making an announcement to open Senate hearings) Are we all ready? What is now amiss that Caesar and his Senate must redress?

Casca: (Giving the signal) Speak, hands, for me.

(He stabs Caesar in the neck, and the others close in, each striking several blows and pasting "blood" on Caesar's robe. Brutus is last, and the others step aside as approaches.)

Caesar: (Saying, "You too, Brutus?") Et tu, Brute? *(He covers his face. Brutus stabs him. Caesar lowers his cloak and chokes out the next words.)* Then fall, Caesar. *(He dies at the base of Pompey's statue while the conspirators shout.)*

(The crowd runs this way and that, horrified.)

Cinna: Liberty! Freedom! Cry it about the streets.

Cassius: Cry out, "Liberty, freedom, and enfranchisement!"

Brutus: (Trying to quiet the mob.) People and Senators, be not affrighted. Stand still!

Cassius: (Seeing Trebonius enter) Where is Antony?

Trebonius: Fled to his house, amazed. Men, wives, and children stare, cry out, and run as it were doomsday.

Brutus: (To the other conspirators) Stoop, Romans, stoop, and let us bathe our hands in Caesar's blood up to the elbows, and besmear our swords. *(He stoops and puts "blood" on his arms.)* Then walk we forth even to the marketplace, and let's all cry, "Peace, freedom, and liberty!"

Cassius: Ay, every man away. Brutus shall lead. *(All "wash" their hands in Caesar's blood, just as Calpurnia's dream predicted.)*

Brutus: (Looking off, he sees Antony enter.) Here comes Antony. Welcome, Mark Antony. *(The others stand and watch Antony suspiciously.)*

Announcer 2: Here is the difficult part of the assassination, because Antony was Caesar's best friend. If Antony joins them, they are safe. If not, there is trouble ahead.

Antony: (Going to the corpse of Caesar, he looks at it sadly.) O mighty Caesar! Dost thou lie so low? Are all thy conquests, glories, triumphs, spoils shrunk to this little measure? Fare thee well!

Brutus: (As frightened citizens rush by, he speaks to Antony in a kind voice.) Only be patient, and we will deliver you the cause why I, that did love Caesar when I struck him, have thus proceeded.

Antony: (Very quietly) I doubt not of your wisdom. *(He pretends to join them.)* Let each man render me his bloody hand. First, Marcus Brutus, will I shake with you. *(As he shakes hands, his own hand gets bloody.)* Next, Cassius, do I take your hand. Now, Decius, yours. Yours, Cinna. My valiant Casca, yours. Gentlemen all. *(He looks about, trying to be friends.)* Alas, what shall I say?

Cassius: (In a practical manner) Will you be in number of our friends? Or shall we not depend on you?

Antony: (With great honesty) Therefore I took your hands. Friends am I with you all . . . upon this hope, that you shall give me reasons why and wherein Caesar was dangerous. *(He gives a weak smile.)*

Brutus: Our reasons are full of good regard. You should be satisfied.

Antony: That's all I seek. *(He innocently adds a request.)* And am moreover suitor that I may produce his body to the marketplace and, as becomes a friend, speak in his funeral.

Brutus: (Generously) You shall, Mark Antony.

Announcer 1: Here Brutus makes a second mistake. His first was killing Caesar without a good reason. Now he is going to let Antony make a funeral speech.

Cassius: (Pulling Brutus to one side with a frown) Brutus, a word with you. Do not consent that Antony speak in his funeral.

Brutus: (Quietly overruling Cassius) By your pardon, I will myself into the pulpit first and show the reason of our Caesar's death. What Antony shall speak, I will protest he speaks by permission.

Cassius: (Very alarmed) I like it not.

Brutus: (Shrugging, he returns to the others.) Mark Antony, here, take you Caesar's body. You shall not in your funeral speech blame us, but speak all good you can of Caesar.

Antony: (Meekly) I do desire no more.

Brutus: Prepare the body then and follow us. *(As he and the others exit, Antony's face changes to anger.)*

Announcer 2: Antony now shows his real feelings. He apologizes to Caesar, who was the greatest man in the world. He swears Caesar's ghost will cry for revenge and bloody war.

Antony: (To dead Caesar, with grief) O, pardon me, thou bleeding piece of earth, that I am meek and gentle with these butchers. Thou art the ruins of the noblest man that ever lived in the tide of times.

(Looking after the murderers, he shakes his fist at them in fury.) Woe to the hand that shed this costly blood! A curse shall light upon the limbs of men. *(He points to Caesar, whose ghost will rise.)* And Caesar's spirit, ranging for revenge, come hot from Hell, shall in these confines with a monarch's voice cry, "Havoc!" and let slip the dogs of war that this foul deed shall smell above the earth with carrion men, groaning for burial.

Announcer 1: A messenger arrives from Octavius Caesar, who is Julius Caesar's adopted son.

Antony: You serve Octavius Caesar, do you not?

Servant: I do, Mark Antony. *(He sees the corpse and stops, horrified.)* O Caesar!

Antony: Is thy master coming?

Servant: He lies tonight within seven leagues of Rome.

Antony: Stay awhile. Lend me your hand. *(Together they carry the dead Caesar to the bench at the rear of the stage, covering him with his cloak. The servant leaves, and kneels. Meanwhile Brutus enters, followed by several terrified citizens.)*

Announcer 2: Brutus must calm the people, who are frightened by the murder.

Citizens: (Shouting) We will be satisfied!

Brutus: (Quieting them) Then give me audience, friends. *(He goes behind the scenery and climbs the ladder, appearing above them to speak.)*

Third Citizen: The noble Brutus is ascended. Silence.

Brutus: (In a kind and honest voice) Romans, countrymen and lovers, be silent, that you may hear. Believe me for mine honor. If any dear friend of Caesar's demand why Brutus rose against Caesar, this is my answer: not that I loved Caesar less, but that I loved Rome more. *(The citizens murmur with surprise.)*

As Caesar loved me, I weep for him. As he was fortunate, rejoice at it. As he was valiant, I honor him.

But as he was ambitious, I slew him. *(The crowd nods approval.)* There is tears for his love, joy for his fortune, honor for his valor, and death for his ambition. *(A few cheer.)* I have the same dagger for myself, when it shall please my country to need my death! *(All cheer loudly.)*

All Citizens: Live, Brutus, live, live!

1 Citizen: Bring him with triumph home unto his house.

3 Citizen: Let him be Caesar. *(They all cheer.)*

Brutus: (Calming them) Good countrymen, for my sake, stay here with Antony. Not a man depart, save I alone, till Antony have spoke. *(He gets down and leaves, as Antony climbs up to speak.)*

Announcer 1: The crowd, which loved Pompey and then Caesar and now Brutus, waits to hear Antony speak.

1 Citizen: (With conviction) This Caesar was a tyrant.

3 Citizen: Nay, that's certain. We are blessed that Rome is rid of him.

2 Citizen: Peace, *(He sees Antony trying to quiet them.)* *l*et us hear what Antony can say.

Announcer 2: Antony begins by stating he will only bury his friend, not say how good he was.

Antony: (Sadly) Friends, Romans, countrymen lend me your ears. I come to bury Caesar, not to praise him.

The noble Brutus hath told you Caesar was ambitious. *(He sighs.)* If it were so, it was a grievous fault, and grievously hath Caesar answered it.

(He sighs again, and the citizens begin to feel uncertain about the "if.") He was my friend, faithful and just to me. But Brutus says he was ambitious, and Brutus is an honorable man. *(With grief)* When that the poor have cried, Caesar hath wept! *(Sarcastically)* Yet Brutus says he was ambitious, and Brutus is an honorable man.

Announcer 1: Antony then makes his main point—the crowd saw Caesar refuse the crown three times.

Antony: You all did see that on the Lupercal I thrice presented him a kingly crown, which he did thrice refuse. Was this ambition? *(The citizens shake their heads.)* Yet Brutus says he was ambitious, and sure, he is an honorable man. *(By now the citizens exchange worried looks, as the facts do not make sense.)*

(Pointing to Caesar's corpse) You all did love him once, not without cause. *(He wipes tears from his face.)* Bear with me. My heart is in the coffin there with Caesar, and I must pause till it come back to me. *(He covers his face with his robe.)*

1 Citizen: (Unhappily) Methinks there is much reason in his sayings.

2 Citizen: (Shocked) Caesar has had great wrong.

4 Citizen: Marked ye his words? He would not take the crown, therefore, 'tis certain he was not ambitious. *(The others agree.)*

3 Citizen: There's not a nobler man in Rome than Antony. *(Their minds have changed completely.)*

Antony: (Taking out a scroll sadly) Here's a parchment with the seal of Caesar. 'Tis his will. I must not read it. It is not meet you know how Caesar loved you. 'Tis good you know not that you are his heirs. *(He waves it at them temptingly.)*

4 Citizen: Read the will! We'll hear it, Antony.

Antony: Will you be patient? I fear I wrong the honorable men whose daggers have stabbed Caesar.

4 Citizen: They were traitors. Honorable men?

All Citizens: The will, the testament!

Antony: (Hiding a smile, as the citizens do exactly what he wants.) You will compel me then to read the will? Then make a ring about the corpse of Caesar, and let me show you him that made the will.

(He comes down and stands behind Caesar's body, showing all the cuts in the toga.) If you have tears, prepare to shed them now. *(He points to a bloody slit.)* Look, in this place ran Cassius' dagger through. *(Points to more blood.)* See what a rent the envious Casca made. *(He puts his finger through a hole.)* Through this the well-beloved Brutus stabbed. *(He shouts.)* This was the most unkindest cut of all. Then burst his mighty heart, and even at the base of Pompey's statue, great Caesar fell. *(He whips off Caesar's toga.)* Look you here. Here is himself, marred, as you see, with traitors.

2 Citizen: O noble Caesar!

3 Citizen: O woeful day!

4 Citizen: O traitors, villains!

1 Citizen: O most bloody sight!

All: Revenge! About! Seek! Burn! Fire! Kill! Slay!

Antony: (Trying to calm them) Stay, countrymen. Good friends, sweet friends, let me not stir you up to such a sudden flood of mutiny. *(He points where Brutus left.)* They that have done this deed are honorable. *(He spits in scorn.)*

All Citizens: (Shouting) We'll mutiny.

Antony: Why, friends, you go to do you know not what. You have forgot the will I told you of.

All Citizens: Most true. The will. Let's hear the will.

Announcer 2: Caesar not only left every citizen some money but also left land for a public park.

Antony: (Impressively) Here is the will, and under Caesar's seal, to every Roman citizen he gives seventy-five drachmas. *(He throws them some coins.)* Moreover, he hath left you all his walks and orchards on this side Tiber, to you and your heirs for ever. *(The crowd cheers wildly.)* Here was a Caesar. When comes such another?

1 Citizen: Never, never! Come away, away! We'll burn his body in the holy place. Take up the body. *(They pick up Caesar as they shout.)*

2 Citizen: Go fetch fire!

3 Citizen: Pluck down benches! *(They leave, rioting.)*

Antony: (Watching them and laughing) Now let it work. Mischief, thou art afoot. *(Octavius' servant enters.)* How now, fellow?

Servant: Sir, Octavius is already come to Rome.

Antony: (Excited by his luck) He comes upon a wish.

Announcer 1: There is great news—Brutus and Cassius have fled from the Roman mob.

Servant: I heard him say Brutus and Cassius are rid like madmen through the gates of Rome.

Antony: (With a victory cheer) Bring me to Octavius. *(They leave, sure of success.)*

ACT IV

(The servants remove the statues and bring on several spears propped together. They also bring on a table and two stools and move the bench to the table.)

Announcer 2: Far away from Rome, near the city of Sardis in Turkey, Brutus and Cassius have formed an army. They plan to fight Antony and young Octavius Caesar.

Announcer 1: But already Brutus and Cassius are having a quarrel. Cassius has been taking bribes so he can pay his soldiers in his half of the army.

Brutus and Cassius enter from different sides and meet at the table in anger.)

Cassius: Most noble brother, you have done me wrong. *(He slams his on the table.)* You have condemned Lucius Pella for taking bribes here.

Brutus: (Coldly furious) You wronged yourself to write in such a case. You yourself are much condemned to have an itching palm, to sell and mart your offices for gold.

Cassius: (Exploding with anger) I an itching palm?

Announcer 2: Brutus reminds Cassius that they did not kill Caesar just to become wicked and corrupt.

Brutus: (Nobly) Remember March, the ides of March remember. Did not great Julius bleed for justice' sake? Shall we now contaminate our fingers with base bribes? *(With scorn for his friend)* I had rather be a dog and bay the moon than such a Roman.

Cassius: (Proudly) I am a soldier, I, older in practice, abler than yourself to make conditions.

Brutus: (Equally proud) You are not, Cassius.

Cassius: I am.

Brutus: You say you are a better soldier. *(He laughs mockingly.)* Let it appear so.

Cassius: You wrong me every way *(Confused and unhappy)*. I said an elder soldier, not a better. *(He stops and thinks, shaking his head.)* Did I say better?

Brutus: If you did, I care not. *(He sits, saying in icy tones)* I did send to you for gold to pay my legions, which you denied me. Was that done like Cassius?

Cassius: I denied you not.

Brutus: (Angrily) You did.

Cassius: I did not. *(He blames the messenger.)* He was but a fool that brought my answer back. *(He sits in despair and puts his dagger on the table.)* There is my dagger. *(He jerks apart his robe to bare his chest.)* And here a heart richer than gold. I that denied thee gold will give my heart. Strike as thou didst at Caesar.

Brutus: (Suddenly melting, he says gently,) Sheathe your dagger. *(He pushes the weapon back to Cassius.)* Be angry when you will. Do what you will.

(He puts his hand to his head.) O Cassius, I am sick of many griefs. *(He gives a great sigh.)* Portia is dead.

Cassius: (Shocked) Portia? *(With wonder)* How escaped I killing when I crossed you so?

Brutus: (Bravely) Speak no more of her. *(His servant Lucius brings in a tray with wine, two bowls, a book, and a lighted candle.)* Give me a bowl of wine. *(He and Cassius raise bowls and toast each other.)* In this I bury all unkindness, Cassius. *(They drink.)*

(Leaving the tray on the table, Lucius goes to the door and stands aside as Messala and Titinius enter. Then Lucius sits in the corner and falls asleep.)

Brutus: (Rising to shake hands.) Come in, Titinius. Welcome, good Messala. *(He points to the table and candle.)* Now sit we close about this taper here. *(All sit at the table.)* Messala, I have here received letters that young Octavius and Mark Antony come down upon us with a mighty power, bending their expedition toward Philippi.

Messala: (Pulling out a scroll) Myself have letters of the selfsame tenor.

Announcer 1: Now they must decide where to fight Antony and Octavius—at Philippi, four hundred miles away, or here at Sardis.

Brutus: (To them all) What do you think of marching to Philippi presently?

Cassius: (Sharply) I do not think it good.

Brutus: Your reason?

Announcer 2: Cassius wants the enemy to make the long march here to Sardis, so they will become tired.

Cassius: (Sensibly) Tis better that the enemy seek us. So shall he weary his soldiers, whilst we are of rest, defense, and nimbleness.

Announcer 1: But Brutus wants to make the long march to Philippi. He feels the time is right for them to move, like ships which sail on a high tide to success, not staying trapped in shallow water,

Brutus: Good reasons must of force give place to better. *(Thoughtfully)* There is a tide in the affairs of men which, taken at the flood, leads on to fortune. Omitted, all the voyage of their life is bound in shallows and in miseries. On such a full sea are we now afloat. *(He looks like such a hero that Titinius and Messala agree with him eagerly.)*

Cassius: (Unhappily giving in) Then, go on. We'll along ourselves meet them at Philippi.

Announcer 2: This is Brutus's third mistake—not following Cassius' good military advice.

Brutus: There is no more to say?

Cassius: (Sadly) No more. *(He stands.)* Good night.

Titinius and Messala: Good night, Lord Brutus. *(They rise to leave with Cassius.)*

Brutus: Farewell, every one. *(As they go, Brutus takes up a book.)* Let me see, is not the leaf turned down where I left reading? Here it is, I think.

(As he reads, behind him appears the bloody Ghost of Caesar. Brutus does not see him at first, but he frowns at the candlelight, which grows dim.)

Brutus: How ill this taper burns. *(He sees the Ghost.)* Ha! Who comes here? *(The Ghost approaches him.)* It comes upon me. *(Brutus backs away, frightened.)* Art thou some god, some angel, or some devil, that makest my blood cold? Speak to me what thou art.

Ghost: (In a hollow voice) Thy evil spirit, Brutus.

Brutus: Why comest thou?

Ghost: To tell thee thou shalt see me at Philippi.

Brutus: Well, then I shall see thee again?

Ghost: Ay, at Philippi.

Brutus: (Finding courage) Why, I will see thee at Philippi then. *(The Ghost glides away, as Brutus calls after it.)* Ill spirit, I would hold more talk with thee. *(But the Ghost is gone. Brutus looks around and sees Lucius sleeping. He shakes him.)* Boy, Lucius. Awake! Didst thou see anything?

Lucius: (Sleepily) My lord? *(He starts to rise.)*

Brutus: Go to my brother Cassius. Bid him set on, and we will follow. *(They leave quickly.)*

ACT V

(The servants remove the spears, table, bench and stools. They bring on a large desert rock or two.)

Announcer 1: Brutus and Cassius march four hundred miles to meet Octavius and Antony on the plains of Philippi, halfway between Sardis and Rome.

Brutus and Cassius with their soldiers enter on one side, and Antony and young Octavius with their men on the other. The space between them is empty. All wear appropriate colors.)

Cassius: (To his officer) Stand fast, Titanius. We must out and talk.

Octauius: (To Antony, uncertainly) Mark Antony, shall we give sign of battle?

Antony: (Calmly) No, Caesar.

(To the sound of trumpet or drum, the four generals march to the center.)

Brutus: (To Antony and Octavious) Words before blows. Is it so, countrymen?

Octavius: (With youthful scorn) Not that we love words better, as you do.

Brutus: Good words are better than bad strokes, Octavius.

Antony: (Laughing at him) In your bad strokes, Brutus, you give good words. Witness the hole you made in Caesar's heart, crying, "Long live, hail Caesar."

Octavious: Look, I draw a sword against conspirators. *(He brings out his weapon.)* Come, Antony, away. *(He challenges the others.)* If you dare fight today, come to the field. *(He and and their men leave.)*

Announcer 2: At this point, Brutus and Cassius must decide what they will do if they are defeated.

Cassius: Now, most noble Brutus, if we do lose this battle, then is this the very last time we shall speak together. What are you determined to do?

Announcer 1: Brutus will have two choices, to be paraded in chains as a captive in Rome, which is a great insult, or kill himself.

Announcer 2: The Romans considered suicide very honorable.

Brutus: (Refusing capture) Think not that ever Brutus will go bound to Rome. He bears too great a mind. *(Sadly)* But this same day must end that work the ides of March begun. And whether we shall meet again, I know not. *(He grips Cassius's hand with real friendship.)* Therefore, for ever and for ever farewell, Cassius. If we do meet again, why, we shall smile. If not, why then this parting was well made.

Cassius: For ever and for ever farewell, Brutus. If we do meet again, we'll smile indeed. If not, tis true, this parting was well made. *(He smiles bitterly.)*

(They separate and the war begins. Several soldiers come on from each side. Some of the men are killed and some wounded. The war seems about even.)

Brutus: (Entering with Messala) Ride, ride, Messala, ride. *(He hands him scrolls.)* Give these bills unto the legions on the other side. *(Messala salutes and runs off, while Brutus fights his way offstage.)*

(As Cassius enters with Titinius, two of his soldiers drop their swords and run away. He points angrily.)

Cassius: O, look, Titinius, look: the villains fly.

Pindarus: (Entering with alarm) Fly further off, my lord. Mark Antony is in your tents, my lord. Fly, therefore, noble Cassius, fly far off.

Titinius: (To Cassius, as he leaves to check on the situation) I will be here again even with a thought.

Announcer 1: But Cassius thinks the war is lost.

Cassius: (To Pindarus) Come hither, sirrah. In Parthia did I take thee prisoner. Now be a freeman, and with this good sword, that ran through Caesar's bowels, search this bosom. *(He gives the sword to Pindarus.)* Here, and when my face is covered, as tis now, *(He covers his face with his cloak.)* guide thou the sword. *(Pindarus stabs him, and Cassius sags to the ground, gasping.)* Caesar, thou art revenged, even with the sword that killed thee. *(Pindarus runs off.)*

(Messala and Titinius enter, hunting for Cassius.)

Messala: Where did you leave him? *(He sees Cassius's body.)* Is not that he that lies upon the ground?

Titinius: He lies not like the living. *(He turns Cassius over.)* O my heart! Cassius is no more. *(Messala takes off his helmet in respect.)* The sun of Rome is set. Our day is gone. *(Calling)* Pindarus! Where art thou, Pindarus?

Messala: Seek him, Titinius, whilst I go to meet the noble Brutus. *(He leaves.)*

Titinius: (Taking Cassius's sword) By your leave, gods, this is a Roman's part. Come, Cassius's sword, and find Titinius's heart! *(He stabs himself.)*

Brutus: (Entering with Messala) Where, where, Messala, doth his body lie?

Messala: Lo, yonder. *(He points, and they see that Titinius has committed suicide also.)*

Announcer 2: Brutus realizes that Julius Caesar is still powerful, though dead. His ghost makes them kill themselves.

Brutus: (Looking upwards) O Julius Caesar, thou art mighty yet. Thy spirit walks abroad and turns our swords in our own proper entrails. *(To dead Cassius)* The last of all the Romans, fare thee well. *(To the others)* Come, let us to the field. Tis three o'clock. And, Romans, yet ere night, we shall try fortune in a second fight. *(All leave, taking the bodies.)*

(More fighting continues, but Brutus's troops are either slain or run away. At last Brutus comes on,

tired and hopeless, with his last men—Volumnius, Clitis, and Strato. Strato sits and falls asleep.)

Announcer 1: The war is over. Brutus has lost.

Announcer 2: All that is left for him is death.

Brutus: (To the others) Come, poor remains of friends. Rest on this rock. *(He and the others sit.)* Hark thee, Clitis. *(He whispers to one man.)*

Clitis: (Shocked) What, I, my lord? No, not for all the world. I'd rather kill myself.

Brutus: (To another officer) Come hither, good Volumnius. *(Volumnius moves closer.)*

Volumnius: What says my lord?

Brutus: Why this, Volumnius. The ghost of Caesar hath appeared to me two several times by night. At Sardis once, and this last night, here in Philippi fields. I know my hour is come. *(A last request)* I prithee, hold thou my sword hilts whilst I run on it.

Volumnius: (Shaking his head) That's not an office for a friend, my lord.

Clitis: (Jumping to his feet and pointing off, where an army approaches.) Fly, fly, my lord!

Brutus: (Clasping hands with his good friends for the last time.) Countrymen, my heart doth joy that yet in all my life, I found no man but he was true to me. I shall have glory by this losing day, more than Octavius and Mark Antony. So fare you well. *(He pushes them off gently.)* Hence! I will follow. *(They go, all but Strato, who has waked. Brutus speaks to him urgently.)* Strato, stay thou by thy lord. Hold my sword, and turn away thy face while I do run upon it. Wilt thou, Strato?

Strato: Give me your hand first. *(They clasp hands with emotion.)* Fare you well, my lord.

Brutus: (Looking up to the heavens.) Caesar, now be still. I killed not thee with half so good a will. *(Strato holds the sword; Brutus runs on it and dies. Strato kneels in prayer beside him, as Octavius and Antony enter with their troops.)*

Announcer 1: Antony praises Brutus, the only conspirator who acted for the good of Rome, not out of jealousy of Caesar. In spite of his mistakes, Brutus was the best of the Romans.

Antony: (Kneeling by Brutus with deep respect.) This was the noblest Roman of them all. All the conspirators, save only he, did that they did in envy of great Caesar. *(With admiration)* His life was gentle, and the elements so mixed in him that nature might stand up and say to all the world, "This was a man."

Octavius: (Planning Brutus's funeral) According to his virtue let us use him, with all respect and rites of burial. So call the field to rest, and let's away, to part the glories of this happy day. *(To stately music, all march off, carrying the bodies with them.)*

EPILOGUE

(If desired, the play can explain history further. With this ending, Octavius and Antony alone should stay on stage. Servants remove the rocks and bring back the bench center stage.)

Announcer 2: This is the end of Shakespeare's play.

Announcer 1: However, we thought you might like to know what happened to the real characters in history.

Announcer 2: After the battle of Philippi, Octavius Caesar and Mark Antony shared the leadership of Rome. *(The two men clasp hands.)*

Announcer 1: They decided to go different ways. Octavius returned to Rome to lead the country. *(Octavius goes to one side of the stage, where clerks bring him scrolls that he reads busily, silently dictating answers like a businessman.)*

Announcer 2: Antony went on a tour of the East. *(Antony goes to the other side of the stage, meeting Herod and Cleopatra.)* He visited Herod the Great, King of the Jews. *(He and Herod bow to each other, and Herod strolls off.)* He met with Cleopatra, the Queen of Egypt. *(Cleopatra puts her arm through Antony's. They smile.)*

Announcer 1: Then Antony and Cleopatra wanted to split the Roman government, taking the Eastern part and leaving Octavius the West.

Announcer 2: Octavius refused, which led to a war. *(Octavius gives the clerks his papers and draws his sword. He and Antony cross swords, center stage.)* Octavius won. *(Cleopatra looks frightened and runs away from the fight. Antony joins her. He takes his sword and kills himself. She waves to a servant to bring her a basket of fruit, takes a snake out of the basket, puts it to her heart, and dies. Servants remove the bodies. Octavius returns to his clerks, again busy with paperwork.)*

Announcer 1: Octavius then was crowned the first Roman emperor. The Roman Republic was dead, and the Roman Empire began. Octavius took the name of Augustus Caesar. *(A Roman puts a wreath on his head.)*